Mrs. Maccabee's MIRACLE

For Menachem, who knows that even Maccabees need their mother. The milk is on the top shelf of the fridge, on the right side. —E.W.

To Agathe, Hannah, and Cyril —A.V.

"The Story of Hanukkah" on pages 22-23 by Jacqueline Jules, from *Light the Menorah: A Hanukkah Handbook,* © 2018 Kar-Ben Publishing®

KAR-BEN PUBLISHING®
An imprint of Lerner Publishing Group, Inc.
241 First Avenue North
Minneapolis, MN 55401 USA

Website address: www.karben.com

Main body text set in Athenaeum Std
Typeface provided by Monotype Typography

Library of Congress Cataloging-in-Publication Data

Names: Weber, Elka, 1968– author. | Videlo, Amélie, 1985– illustrator.
Title: Mrs. Maccabee's miracle / Elka Weber ; illustrated by Amélie Videlo.
Description: Minneapolis, MN : Kar-Ben Publishing, [2023] | Audience: Ages 3–8. | Audience: Grades K–1. | Summary: The five Maccabee sons are always losing things, and their mom is ever there to remind them where to look, but when they cannot find the oil to light the Temple menorah after defeating the Greek army, they must remember her sage advice. Includes the story of Hanukkah.
Identifiers: LCCN 2022040489 (print) | LCCN 2022040490 (ebook) | ISBN 9781728477916 (library binding) | ISBN 9781728495347 (ebook)
Subjects: LCSH: Hanukkah—Juvenile fiction. | CYAC: Hanukkah—Fiction. | Jews—Jerusalem—Fiction. | Family life—Jerusalem—Fiction. | Jerusalem—Fiction. | LCGFT: Picture books.
Classification: LCC PZ7.W3876 Mr 2023 (print) | LCC PZ7.W3876 (ebook) | DDC [E]—dc23

LC record available at https://lccn.loc.gov/2022040489
LC ebook record available at https://lccn.loc.gov/2022040490

Manufactured in the United States of America
1-52482-50744-11/28/2022

Mrs. Maccabee's MIRACLE

Elka Weber

illustrated by Amélie Videlo

KAR-BEN
PUBLISHING

The Maccabee house in Modi'in was full of happiness and noise. Mr. and Mrs. Maccabee and their five sons were a jolly, busy family.

A few times a year, the Maccabee men would go to Jerusalem to help in the Holy Temple.

"Mom, have you seen my traveling cloak?"

"Cloaks don't grow legs and walk away. Where you leave them is where they stay."

"I still can't find it."

"On the hook near the window."

"Thanks, Mom."

When the Maccabees weren't helping in the Temple,

they spent their time studying and teaching Torah.

"Mom, have you seen my scroll?"

"Scrolls don't grow legs and walk away.
Where you leave them is where they stay."

"I still can't find it."

"On the table."

"Thanks, Mom."

One day, a Greek kingdom, led by King Antiochus, took over the Land of Israel and passed a law that Jews couldn't study Torah anymore.

But the Jews wanted to keep studying Torah. In order to fool the Greeks, they came up with a plan.

They took their spinning tops with them whenever they studied. If they saw a Greek soldier who might suspect they were studying, they quickly took out their spinning tops and pretended they were just playing a game.

"Mom, have you seen my spinning top?"

"Tops don't grow legs and walk away. Where you leave them is where they stay."

"I still can't find it."

"In the box under your bed."

"Thanks, Mom."

The Greeks made life harder and harder for the
Jews. Finally, the Jews decided to fight back.

"Mom, have you seen my spear?"

"Spears don't grow legs and walk away.
Where you leave them is where they stay."

"I still can't find it."

"Next to the door."

"Thanks, Mom."

The Maccabees fought very bravely. Although they were only a small army, they beat the mighty Greeks.

As soon as the final battle was over, the Maccabees went straight to the Temple in Jerusalem. Their first task was to find a jug of oil to relight the great menorah.

But the Greeks left a big mess, and the Maccabees couldn't find the oil anywhere. They looked, they searched, and they hunted, but without luck.

"What would Mom say?" they asked each other.

And they could hear her voice saying, "Jugs of oil don't grow legs and walk away. Where you leave them is where they stay."

Lo and behold, they remembered where they'd
last seen the little jug of oil before the great battle.
There wasn't much oil left in the jug—just enough
to last for a day.

But when they relit the menorah, the flames burned not for just one day but for eight whole days!

Every year in the happy, noisy house in Modi'in, Mrs. Maccabee
would tell the story of Hanukkah to her jolly, busy family.

"And then the Maccabees found a small jug of oil to light
the menorah," she would say, nodding at the twinkling lights.
"Without my help."

"Indeed!" she would say.

"A great miracle happened here."

The Story of Hanukkah

Over two thousand years ago, a king named Antiochus controlled Israel. Antiochus was powerful and ruthless. He wanted all of the people under his rule to abandon their own religious practices to follow the customs of Greek culture. Antiochus denied Jews the right to observe Shabbat, Jewish holidays, Jewish dietary laws, and other important Jewish rituals. It became dangerous for people to even identify themselves as Jewish. Some Jews adopted Greek culture and religion. They stopped studying Torah and observing the Sabbath. But other Jews did not give up their heritage and religion.

Strong resistance rose up in the countryside, particularly in Modi'in, a town west of Jerusalem where a priest named Mattathias lived with his five sons. Mattathias was well-respected. The king's soldiers wanted him to be the first to step forward and show loyalty to King Antiochus. Mattathias answered loudly and clearly. He would not worship idols or forsake Judaism. With his sons by his side, Mattathias fled to the mountains to organize a revolt against Antiochus. When Mattathias died, he turned over his leadership to his son, Judah. Judah's bold fighting style earned him the nickname "Maccabee," meaning "hammer." Judah, his brothers, and growing band of followers waged war against Antiochus. They were called the Maccabees and they found success through night raids and sneak attacks. Their courage fighting a large and well-equipped army inspired Jews all over the country. In one famous battle, the Maccabees even faced soldiers who were riding trained war elephants.

In 164 BCE, after three years of fighting, the Maccabees gained control of the Temple in Jerusalem. This was as much a spiritual victory as a military one. Now the Jews could rededicate their most sacred house of worship. The Temple and its grounds were in terrible condition. The sanctuary was filthy. Ornate doors had been burned.

The golden menorah that once burned with seven branches of continuous torch light was gone. The Maccabees tore their clothing as a sign of mourning. They wailed and wept. Then they got to work. First, they scrubbed the Temple from sstop to bottom. They pulled weeds and made repairs. Some sources say the Maccabees made a makeshift menorah from iron spears. Others say a gold seven-branched lamp was created. On the twenty-fifth day of the Hebrew month of Kislev, the new menorah was lit and the Temple was rededicated. In Hebrew, the word "Hanukkah" means "dedication." The very first Hanukkah lasted eight days, just like the fall harvest holiday of Sukkot. During wartime, the Maccabees couldn't take a week to observe Sukkot properly, so they celebrated for eight days during the rededication of the Temple. This is the historical view of the first Hanukkah holiday.

However, rabbinic tradition gives another reason for the eight-day celebration. It was said that the Maccabees needed oil to light the menorah. They searched the Temple. All they found was one small cruse of sealed, purified oil—only enough to last one day. Instead of delaying their ceremony for eight days until more oil could be obtained, the Maccabees lit the menorah anyway. Miraculously, the small amount of oil burned for eight full days. This legend, known as the "miracle of the oil," encourages us to remember a triumph of faith along with a military conquest. When we light Hanukkah candles, we are celebrating religious freedom. We are sharing a belief that determined individuals can successfully fight for justice. Hanukkah is also called "The Festival of Lights." May the light of freedom always burn brightly in our homes and in our hearts.

About the Author

When Elka Weber is not busy serving as her family's finder-in-chief, she writes for children and adults. Her books include *The Yankee at the Seder, One Little Chicken,* and *Shimri's Big Idea.* She lives in Israel.

About the Illustrator

Amélie Videlo was born in Paris in the Year of the Rat. While growing up, she lived in France and the Republic of Mauritius. She is a graduate of the Penninghen School of Art Direction and lives in the British countryside, close to the Welsh mountains, with her partner and her cat Chichi. Her preferred mediums are paints, crayons, inks, and digital applications.